Maggie and Pie
and the Pizza Party

By Carolyn Cory Scoppettone
Art by Paula J. Becker

HIGHLIGHTS PRESS
Honesdale, Pennsylvania

Stories + Puzzles = Reading Success!

Dear Parents,

Highlights Puzzle Readers are an innovative approach to learning to read that combines puzzles and stories to build motivated, confident readers.

Developed in collaboration with reading experts, the stories and puzzles are seamlessly integrated so that readers are encouraged to read the story, solve the puzzles, and then read the story again. This helps increase vocabulary and reading fluency and creates a satisfying reading experience for any kind of learner. In addition, solving puzzles fosters important reading and learning skills such as:

- shape and letter recognition
- letter-sound relationships
- visual discrimination
- logic
- flexible thinking
- sequencing

With high-interest stories, humorous characters, and trademark puzzles, Highlights Puzzle Readers offer a winning combination for inspiring young learners to love reading.

This is Maggie.

This is Pie.

Maggie and Pie love to cook. But sometimes Maggie gets a little **mixed up**.

You can help by using the clues to find the supplies they need.

Happy reading!

The sun shines on a ripe red tomato.

"That tomato makes me hungry," says Maggie. "Hungry for pizza!"

"Yum," says Pie. "Here is a recipe. First, we need a ball of dough."

"I can get it," says Maggie.

"Why did you get that?" asks Pie.

"You said we need a ball," says Maggie.

"Oh no," sighs Pie.

"We need a *dough* ball,

not a *basketball*!"

"The pizza dough is in the fridge.

It is on the top shelf.

It is round.

It is the biggest thing on that shelf.

Can you find it?" asks Pie.

"Here is the dough!" says Maggie.

"Thanks," says Pie.

"Now we stretch the dough."

"I will be right back!" says Maggie.

"What are you wearing?" asks Pie.

"This is what I wear to stretch," says Maggie.

"Oh no," sighs Pie.

"*We* are not stretching.

We are stretching the *dough*."

"Next, we need sauce.

It is in a yellow can.

It is on the same shelf as the cookies.

It is to the left of the pasta.

Can you find it?" asks Pie.

"Here is the sauce!" says Maggie.

"Thanks," says Pie.

"Next, we need to grate some cheese."

"I can get it," says Maggie.

"These are all great," says Maggie.

"I could not make up my mind."

"Oh no," sighs Pie.

"We will use a grater to cut the cheese."

"The grater is pink.

It is on the middle shelf.

It is next to the mixer.

It is not next to the teapot.

Can you find it?" asks Pie.

"Here is the grater!" says Maggie.

"Thanks," says Pie.
"Next, we need some peppers.
They are in a basket in the garden."

"I can get it," says Maggie.

"I found the basket," says Maggie.

"But I don't see any peppers."

"Not *that* basket, Maggie!" sighs Pie.

"The peppers are over there."

"Here are the peppers!" says Maggie.

"Thanks," says Pie.
"The pizza is almost ready to bake.
We just need a little olive oil."

"I can get it!" says Maggie.

"Here is a little olive," says Maggie.

"And here is the oil."

"Oh no," sighs Pie.

"The olive oil is in a green bottle.

It is next to a white box.

It is under a pink box.

Can you find it?" asks Pie.

"Here is the olive oil!" says Maggie.

"Thanks," says Pie.

"Now we pour the olive oil . . ."

"Poor olive oil? Did it get hurt?"
asks Maggie.

"We POUR the olive oil," Pie says.

"That's how we get it on the pizza."

"Oh!" says Maggie.

"Why didn't you say that?"

"Time to bake the pizza," says Pie.

"Not yet," says Maggie.

"We need to add the olives

to make this a party."

"How will olives make this a party?" asks Pie.

"The olives are the eyes.

This pepper is the mouth.

And this pepper is the nose.

Now we have a friend," says Maggie.

"And now it is a party!" says Pie.

"After we eat our yummy pizza,
we can play basketball!" says Maggie.

Funny-Face Pizzas

Wash your hands or wings!

You Need

- Cooking spray
- Red bell pepper
- Pizza dough
- Round glass or cookie cutter
- Pizza sauce
- Grated cheese
- Sliced black olives

1. Spray.

Spray a **baking sheet** with **cooking spray**.

2. Slice.

Slice a **red bell pepper** into thin curvy strips.

Ask an adult for help with anything sharp!

3. Cut.

Cut the **pizza dough** into small circles with an upside-down **glass** or **cookie cutter**. Put them on the baking sheet.